Go to School, Little Monster

by **Helen Ketteman**   illustrated by **Bonnie Leick**

two lions

two lions

Published by Two Lions, New York

www.apub.com

Amazon, the Amazon logo, and Two Lions are trademarks of
Amazon.com, Inc., or its affiliates.

Library of Congress Control Number: 2014915912

ISBN-13: 9781477826362
ISBN-10: 147782636X

The illustrations are rendered in watercolor.
Book design by Merideth Mulroney and Vera Soki

Printed in China
First Edition

For Jackie and Ray, Helen, Jamie, Heather, Kaylee, and Will—H. K.

For my mom, Mary— the great cultivator of many little monsters—B. L.

Welcome, Little Monster,
to your first day of school.
I am your teacher.
My name's Mr. Drool.

Don't hang back, Little Monster.
Come in. Don't be shy.
Though I'm big and I drool,
I'm a fairly nice guy.

Take that seat, Little Monster—
the one on Fang's right.

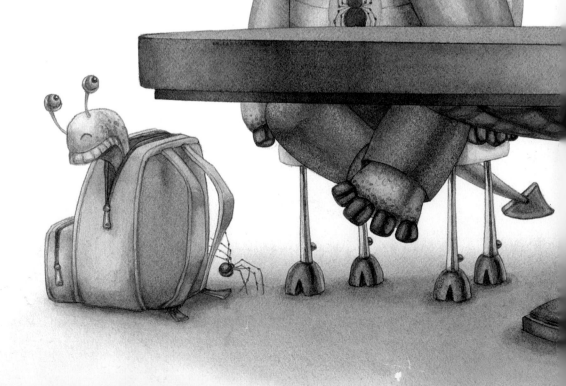

Yes, his teeth are quite big,
but I don't think he'll bite.

Time for art, Little Monster.
What did Fang draw?
A huge dinosaur
with you in its jaw!

Don't fret, Little Monster.
It's only pretend.
I think Fang is saying
he wants to be friends.

Recess, Little Monster!
Go play outside.
The playground has ogres
and dragons to ride.

Good choice, Little Monster!
The dragons are fun.
Be sure to hold on—
they do like to run!

Recess is over.
It's time now to read.
This story, you'll find,
is quite fun indeed.

Here's the book, Little Monster.
Its name is *Stomp Song*.
So listen and stomp
as I read along.

Lunch time Little Monster!
What did you bring?
Oh, dear! You forgot?
You don't have a thing?

Don't feel so bad.
No need to despair.
Fang has a huge lunch,
and he wants to share.

Don't be scared, Little Monster,
to try something new.
That's good. Take a piece.
Now bite down and chew!

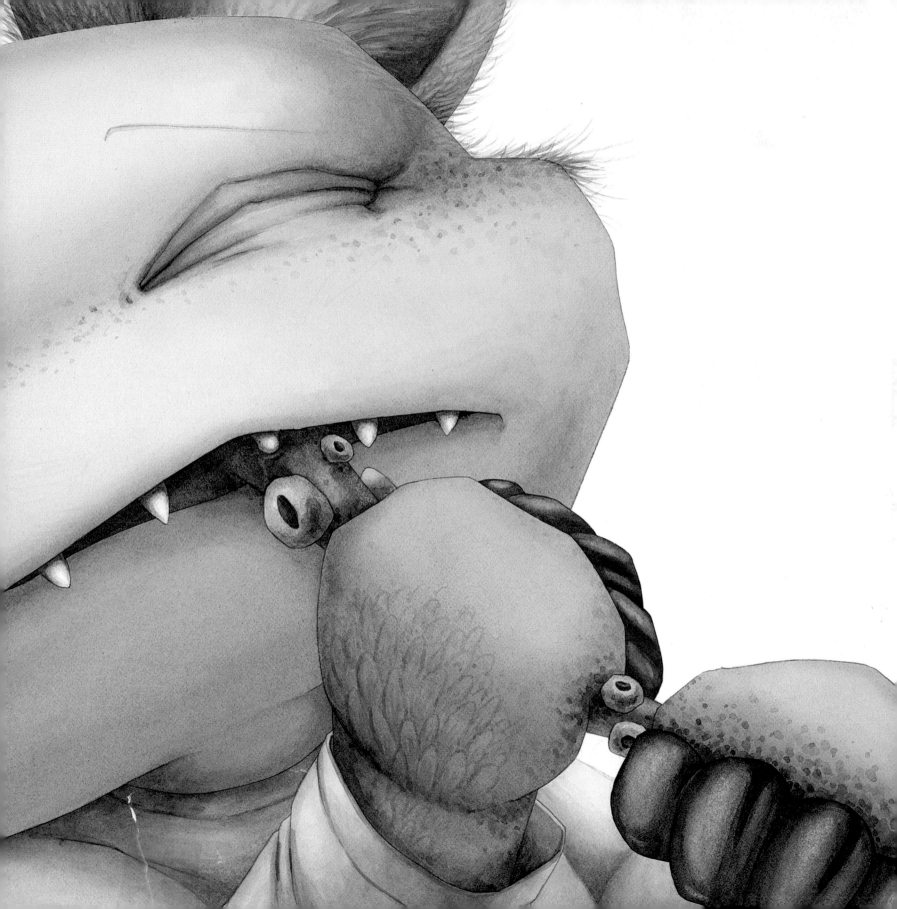

You like it, Little Monster?
I thought that you would!

It may be different,
but different is good.

Math time, Little Monster.
Point here, count out loud
the number of demons
that make up the crowd.

Uh-oh, Little Monster.
I think you missed one.
You and Fang count together.
Yes! That's how it's done!

Show-and-tell, Little Monster.
You have something to say?
You've made a new friend
on your very first day!

Don't be sad, Little Monster,
that our day's at an end.
You'll be back tomorrow . . .

to see your new friend!